Published by The Tyson Collection, Atlanta Georgia.

ISBN: 978-1-967527-12-0
First Edition

Printed in the United States of America

Book I of the Encore Series

The Moth House

Stories of Mental Health, Resilience, and Transformation

Fourteen Seconds

The Day the Bronx Stopped Believing

Tony had the ball with fourteen seconds left, and I already knew we were going to lose.

Not because Westview's defense was better—they weren't. Not because we were down by five—Tony had come back from worse. I knew because of the way he was breathing. Ragged. Desperate. Like someone who'd been up until 3 AM at Vanessa's house instead of sleeping. Again.

My best friend. Tony Carlisle. The guy who'd dropped forty-one points in a single game as a sophomore. Six-foot-four with a wingspan like a pterodactyl and handles so smooth he made defenders look like they were standing still. Pass him the ball from beyond the arc and the whole team would just turn and run—routine. Before I could even cross half court, there'd be that swish, that roar, Tony already jogging back on defense like it was nothing.

We'd gone undefeated all season—ranked number one in the country with a perfect record. This was our chance to leave our mark on the walls of high school basketball history. College recruiters had been calling his house for months, offering all-expense-paid campus tours. UConn. Syracuse. Maryland. They all wanted him.

But that was before the parties. Before the girls. Before the drugs. Before Tony succumbed to the allure of being a local star, blurring the edges of his reality. Before Vanessa trailed her hand down his chest and whispered about "taking a different kind of shot." Before Tony started missing practice, showing up late with that cocky grin: I'm still better than everybody in our division.

I'd ruptured my Achilles second game of the season, and maybe that's why I saw it all so clearly from the bench. I couldn't play anymore—couldn't do anything but watch. I used to tell Tony he'd be the one to make it to the NBA. I was honest about my abilities. I just wanted to run a state-of-the-art sports rehab facility someday. But Tony? Tony was supposed to be our golden ticket out of the Bronx.

Except now he was blinded by his own shine.

Fourteen seconds. The National High School Championship Invitational. Every scout in the region packed into these stands, notebooks open. This was supposed to be Tony's coronation. His destiny.

Coach called our last timeout. Tony jogged to the bench, grabbed a towel, wiped the sweat. But underneath? Pure frustration. I could see it in his eyes—that same look from three nights ago.

THREE NIGHTS EARLIER

Tony and I were sitting on Vanessa's couch, vibing with the most popular girls in the city. Her parents were always on some work-cation, so she had the official hangout spot— strictly invite-only, but somehow always packed. The Game's "Higher" came on and Tony jumped up. "Turn this up! This song puts me in my zone!" He started rapping along, hyping up the whole room. Everyone joined in, shouting the chorus. When it ended, the place erupted—applause, cheers, the works.

I tapped his arm with a bottle of water. "My man! You've been killing it on the court lately."

His attention was locked on Vanessa, but he managed to respond. "Thanks, man. The whole team is stepping up this season."

Vanessa leaned in close. "Leave the basketball talk for the locker room. I'm throwing a special party later tonight."
Tony raised an eyebrow. "Party? Tonight? Coach will kill me if I miss practice again."

She smiled, trailing her hand down his chest. "Practice? You're Tony Carlisle. The scouts are already eyeing you. You're probably going to get drafted before you finish college. One night off won't hurt."

"I don't know, bro," I tried to intercept, weak as it was. "You've already missed the first half of our last few practices. Coach has been pushing us harder lately."

Vanessa leaned in closer, her voice dropping to a seductive whisper. "Maybe later you can take a different kind of shot."

Tony stuttered like a fumbled dribble. "I—I guess one more night won't hurt. I've been on fire lately." She ran her hand up his chest, resting it on his lips, pulling his bottom lip down before releasing it. I was caught in a trance, like it was happening to me.

Tony looked over at me, trying to regain his composure. "I'll be out by midnight and show up to practice early tomorrow. Besides, without practice I'm still better than everybody in our division."

Vanessa raised her cup with perfect form. "That's the spirit! Let's make it a night to remember."

Loud cheers. I said nothing.

I should've said more.

*

The timeout ended. Tony walked back onto the court, and the gym exploded—our fans desperate, their fans smelling blood.

Westview doubled him immediately. Aggressive. Denying him the ball. He'd only managed eleven points the entire game. Tony Carlisle. Eleven points. It was impossible to see over him on most nights, impossible to get a shot off when he was locked in. But tonight? Tonight he looked lost.

A teammate—Marcus, our backup guard—set a pick, creating just enough space. The ball found Tony's hands.

Eight seconds.

He squared up from beyond the arc. This was his spot. His soul. I'd seen him drain this shot a thousand times. As a freshman, Coach had let him start as point guard for both the Freshman and JV teams—called it conditioning. Tony had been an absolute force. Offensive playmaking finesse and the kind of aggressive defense that shook fear into rivals. But that was then.

Seven seconds.

His legs weren't underneath him. His form was off—rushed, unbalanced. The defender closed hard.

Six seconds.

Tony released it anyway. Forced it. The ball left his hands flat. No arc. Already drifting left.

Five seconds.

I watched it—the rotation wrong, the trajectory doomed—and felt my chest tighten.

Four seconds. It clanged off the rim so hard the backboard shook.

Three seconds. Westview grabbed the rebound.

Two seconds. Their point guard dribbled out the clock.

One second.

Buzzer.

Game over. National title—gone.

The Westview side erupted. Our side went silent, then the boos started. Slow at first, building into a wave. I watched the scouts close their notebooks, heading for the exits. Watched Coach Miller's face shift from shock to something worse—grief. Watched Tony just standing there at the three-point line, hands on his knees, staring at nothing.

The crowd's adoration transmuted into a chorus of disappointment. Everything we'd worked for—every record Tony had broken, every late-night practice, every sacrifice—it all unraveled in that single moment.

Then Tony moved. He walked to the sideline, bent down, and grabbed the game ball. He turned, his face twisted with rage and frustration, and launched it across the court.

The ball rocketed through the air and smashed directly into Westview's point guard—square in the face.

The crack echoed through the gym. Blood. Everywhere. The kid dropped like a stone, clutching his nose, screaming. Medical staff rushed onto the court. Parents jumped from the stands. Chaos.

Tony didn't run. Didn't move. Just stood there, chest heaving, staring at what he'd done.

I tried to get up—busted Achilles and all—but Coach held me back. "Don't," he said quietly.

The kid's nose was fractured. Clean break. His family, somehow, gracefully chose not to press charges. But it didn't matter.

Every recruiter had already left. Every opportunity—gone. The threads of Tony's once-legendary narrative frayed under the weight of complacency and distraction.

Tony grabbed a towel and covered his face. His world was unraveling. The game was unrelenting, and it cared not for past glories. That one missed week of practice had become the chink in his armor. It was a stark reminder that even the most gifted must never forget the value of discipline and dedication.

In the locker room afterward, Tony sat alone in the corner, still in his uniform, staring at the floor. I limped over on my crutches and sat down next to him.

And I'd watched it happen. Helpless on this bench with my wrapped knee, knowing it was coming.

Because I'd seen him make the wrong choice every single time. The parties. The girls. The distractions. The arrogance. He had the court at his feet, the game in his hands, the future wide open.

And he chose everything else.
This wasn't even the first time I'd tried to warn him.

When the buzzer echoed
Some shots, once missed, can't
be taken again.
But the real game?

That's the one you play when
the crowd's gone silent.

Check!

Midnight Pickup

Under project buildings,
Under flickering street lights,
Under the bridge,
Move fast Pigeons like to shit at night.
Over the train tracks.
Turn left at the bodega.
Papi kept his store open late just to serve us up a hot plate.
He doesn't understand ¿Por qué jugamos juegos en la noche?
It's not just a game, it's rhythm,
Es una conversación con Dios
Every bounce,
El pulso de una generación
The soundtrack of the streets.
The culture
The crossover
The sneakers screech over the hot concrete.
The net stripped from two summers ago,
Everyone still remembers that game.
Respect is earned by how hard you play.
Beefs were squashed on the court.
The sweat.
The competition.
The rim vibrating after a slam dunk.
They're not just chasing a win; it's the feeling
The rush of adrenaline that only ignites night.
The court.
The arena.
The battleground
The sanctuary.

Renewal

In the sprint of life's challenges,
A fast break to redemption,
Accepts all challengers who dare to outrun their past,
and embrace the rhythm of renewal.

Deprivation of Sleep

Deprivation of sleep never stopped me from dreaming.
Whenever I'm awake, I'm still battling my demons.
I'm on a mission,
My engine is steaming,
On the track to success,
Trained to this reason.

I have a write to live,
Write to be heard.
If it's spoken its priceless,
That be my word.
My mind told me to envision a star,
I gauged my eyes out and made them watch me.
Deprivation of sleep never stopped me from dreaming.
Dreaming will never stop me from achieving.

Gave my mouth a paintbrush to speak with,
My canvas is the wind.
Watch me paint portraits in the eyes of tornados.
Make butterflies freeze in mid-air.
Watch wingless birds take flight.
I breed miracles every time I write.

I'm hotwired,
No one to feed me lines, I wrote this.
Swallowed hand grenades for breakfast,
Whenever I spit it's explosive.

I was born to do this.
Sometimes my words are ruthless.
I spit so hard it's like I'm toothless.
I bottled creativity to quench my thirst.
Write until my left-hand cramps and hurts,

But I could never have arthritis.

I could never be too off to write this.

Hear my word,
Upon concrete conversations.
A walking metaphor!
I boiled my teardrops with the fire that fuels my spirit.
Used left over salt to add flavor to Jesus' last supper.
Manipulation,
My rhymes drop like precipitation.
Flow so demanding,
I could make the dead give me a standing ovation.

Ever Never Forever

Ever told yourself you were favored and believed it?
Walk away from a blessing every time you receive it?
Ever convinced yourself that there was something left behind that
you...
Ever felt like you needed?
Ever more than breathing?
Bound to love, made for it.
Sold your future to your past but still not properly paid for it.
Ever a slave for it?
Ever begged for it?
Yearn for it,
Ever not learn from it?
Ever Never Forever

Ever explored it but didn't scratch the surface?
Ever skipped your turn for it?
I mean fell in line until it was your time for it.
Ever pressed your luck for it,
Told yourself you were done but then been stuck for it?
Ever Never Forever.

Relationship status? complicated.
Ever primed, prepped your regrets - then ate it?
Ever was too smart to get played but got played anyway?
Knew better you just didn't do better.
Ever have nobody left to blame but you?
Ever kept taking care of everybody but you?

Life in limbo.
Always someone to care for,
Some way to bare more,
Some place wanting you there more,
Than your own shore,

Then you unsure of your own shore
if you own shore
are you sure?
Ever Never Forever.

Cast Away

The challenges increase,
The balance remains.
Fall in love with peace,
Cast away the pain.

Redemption

Lips recovered from a fumbled kiss,
Yet still enough matches to spark.
Our tongues slow dance,
A chance to kindle in the dark.
From that misfire, sparked a desire,
Burning fire.
Redeeming passion with each touch,
Hearts hurry to no rush.
Turning stumbles into a lustful play,
With lips entwined, we rewrite our chapter.
Redemption found in words we do not say.
In every breath, happily ever after.

Hoop Dreams

We stay where shadows play,
Beneath the hoop dreams take flight.
Sneakers on the asphalt sway,
Hopes rise high in the shade of night.
A wandering boy looks lost in a distant glance.
I dribble prayers to the pavement that he finds his way.
Every crossover, a tale unfolds,
Aspirations shimmer like gold,
Hoop dreams, the story told.

The Saga of William

Wounds to Wisdom

The pains of a daunting past can be as horrific as the wind of a winter storm. Those memories can pierce you sharp as if mother nature scorned. Too much exposure to the freezing air can cause frostbite. Bad memories can make you shiver, ripping away warmth. It could leave your heart glaciated, stiff, comatose.

Have you ever felt yourself forgetting how to feel?
That's the oxymoron of a broken heart. The subject's name is not nearly as important as the reason for his departure. He is everyone and no one. I've seen his face in a thousand mirrors in my lifetime, yet he remains amongst the thousands of strangers that I've always never known.

On one of the hottest days of the year, two days after the anniversary of America's independence, William celebrates his Fifteenth Birthday. He rushed down strawberry pancakes, scrambled eggs, and two strips of bacon as if he was an expert at not wasting anything on his clothing. After all, he had to stay clean today. Most of his clothing was hand-me-downs from his older brother. He wore a white polo shirt two sizes too big, jean shorts that cut off just below the knee and his only pair of white name brand sneakers. He tried his best to scrub them decently.

He was barely presentable but William was overwhelmed with excitement because his godfather, who he had not seen in twelve years, picked today to take him shopping. There weren't any men close enough to know about a birthday but he wanted to spend time and money.

Memories of his godfather were dim, fleeting moments on random days where a gift of a dollar was enough to make young William smile.

His mother battled a lifelong drug addiction and was incapable of providing a proper home. To avoid losing her children to foster care, William's grandmother assumed full custody of her five grandchildren.

She raised them as best as poverty would allow, but never allowed anyone in her household to believe that they were poor. She would often say, as long as there's a roof over your head and food on the table, you are better off than most. Some people have it worse than you so be thankful.

William's bedroom faced the front of the house. From the second floor bedroom window, he watched a frail man walk up the steps. William sprang to his feet and checked the time on his new digital watch, a gift from his grandmother.

It's 10:06 am William shouted, "He's early!"

When he stepped out to the porch, the sun beamed directly into his eyes, blocking him from getting a good look at the man.

"Where are we going?" he asked, as they made their way down the street.

"We are going to see some family and then I'm taking you shopping" He stopped walking and removed his shades, giving William a better look at his face. "You do know who I am, don't
You?"

"Yes my godfather," he assured while taking the given time to observe the man as he was preparing for a quiz.

The man stood shy of 6 feet tall. His skin hugged his bones close like a withered rose. The left corner of his black and red baseball cap had dots of gray paint. His hat was pulled down low, covering the abandoned garden in his face. His mustache and beard untamed, long overdue for a shave. He was missing a few front teeth. His smile made William think; he must have had a hard life. He is rather skinny for an old man. His eyes are heavily wet. If he blinks too hard, he will cry.

"No, I'm your father!" The man immediately pulled his shades back over his eyes but still felt the burning stare of his son.

His nerves blended perfectly with his antsy posture.

Somehow, he managed to envelope his guilt in a mailroom of unsorted emotions.

They continued walking but that was the last time William remembered how to feel. He felt his soul jump out of his flesh, run down the block and around the corner. He felt his lungs expand, felt his body fighting against gravity, felt his heart, a war drum before battle. He felt until he could no longer feel.

He blinked, beneath his lids were spent shotgun shells, hollowed with a growing stench that something was rotting there. He tried to find tears but they too left. A battlefield barren!

William woke up the next morning after a dreamless night. He noticed a familiar abandoned feeling, though this time not people but pain was absent. He grabbed his swiss-blade from between his mattress. He sat bedside and thought of the lies that everyone kept for all of those years. He opened the blade in his left hand, made a fist with his right hand while squeezing the knife inside.

Why didn't they just tell the truth?
Why did they make me believe this?
What else are they hiding?

Images flashed in his head of his mother, his grandmother, and then everyone who must have known long before he did, and then his mind jumped to the man claiming to be his father - and then nothing.

He interrupted his thoughts with a deem-welled laughter that weakened into a chuckle by the time it surfaced. He looked down and noticed blood dripping on the floor. He stood in front of the vanity mirror, grabbed a towel from his dresser and pressed it against the cut.

Wow, "that's too funny," pushing the words through his smile.

"Yeah it is!" His reflection answered, smiling back at him. That was the first time he spoke to himself, Deciding never to trust anyone else. He vowed never to be the veil.

William warmly embraced his winter of a reputation. Everywhere he traveled, trailed a path of destruction. He never stayed in one place too long, mastering the art of ending relationships without solid reason. He distanced himself from everyone.

When he had learned of a death in his family, he attended the funeral emotionlessly, alone in a crowded room. The compelling voice that breached his subconscious, argued that there was enough space in the casket for him.

This is just the tip of the iceberg of issues responsible for the monster that William has become. Before he was able to hurt anyone else, he sent himself away, dormant - into the bitter hibernal night.

He offered me a gift, a life free from his torment. A heart rescued from hypothermia, thawed under a once forbidden summer sun. His only wish was to be left alone. I received his gift and vowed to never contact him again. The damage remains.

These are the stories left
behind from a blizzard of a
man, with a penchant to
leave muddy footprints
on fresh snow.

Where Are You?

I am the son of a hustler,
The grind is in my bloodline.
My dad is in the darkness,
He needs to see his son shine.

Many nights I break day,
So that he can see his sun rise.
Now I know why they say it hurts,
To stare into the sun - eyes.
.
Sometimes the truth hides,
Tucked behind the sun's lies.
Supposed to provide heat,
But it's the coldest winter outside.

When outside is really inside, my insides turned out.
My heart used to be your residency,
But you were casted out.
I'm not a wizard but I'm trying to cast as a spell,
"D -A - D" back in again.

I'm losing love dad and I need you to teach me how to win again.
How to navigate through life in this multiverse we're living in.
On different planets dad but you don't have to be my alien.

Just trade in your space-ship for a relationship.
Memories sparkle like stars in my eyes and you can take a grip.
If love is a gun, then I need you to reload it quick,
Take shots at your son, because I can't live like this.

ARTiculate

Turned my speech to strokes,
The wind, a silent painter
Language of my soul.

Family First

My grandmother raised five grandchildren on a prayer and miracle.
We were so poor that the roaches paid rent.
Birthday presents were hand-me-downs.
Christmas presents were wrapped in newspaper.

'Be grateful for what you have, some wish they'd have this'.
Barely any help, she took what she could get.
First of the month checks were blessings from heaven.

My grandmother used the Family First Card like a weapon.
Finding coupons to slash the prices,
Shielding us from starvation.
Even though we were stretched,
She would make miracles in the kitchen.
Made sure we all ate together,
But she served her family first.
Allowed us to have second helpings,
There wasn't always enough to go around.
I can't count the number of meals you missed,
The number of prayers you said,
Before we broke bread.

I saw you look at us as if watching us eat made you full.
You served your family first.
I would offer you my plate,
Tell you I could miss a meal,
But you wouldn't hear of it.
Served your family first.
 Disciplined.

Put your family first, card.
Missed meals, hard.
Midnight prayers, God.
Welcoming arms, healed scars.

You corrected us when we were wrong, told us not to worry.
Your porch light shined bright like opening arms, until we all came home.
Never turned your children away, you taught us,
Put your family first.

I never understood where you learned to be so loving,
Honest, wise, strong, until I picked up a bible.

All the silent sessions,
The midnight prayers,
The faith in the scriptures
The sacrifice
You Grandma,
You.

Addicted

We both started around the same time.
Shifted precision, blurred vision,
Couldn't resist the tempting lines.
You and I-
Numbed the affliction.
Chasing the high.
Bloodshot red in you-I,
See demons creeping beside your bed at night
Frantic, your body panics, a wild boar.
Mimicking your body, shocked my body, springboard.
Collision, head on collision, my condition,
You needed drugs, I wrote the prescriptions
We used to connect the dots and trace lines together
Now you can't connect the dots, forgot how to keep your line
together.
For every agent that scribbled the dots and colored on top of the
colors on page,
Lines knotted, plots-twisted, gifts shifted inside your brain,
My pen adjacent, sacred scriptures hidden inside my veins
Addicted to write, you played chicken with death, ain't feel no pain
The chains remain, cell-blocked, we boxed the same
The demons in plain, still screaming in sync
I write like I can bring back life through ink.

Isolation, still every night a thousand faces
No social life, I use my addiction to replace it.
I write back words
The chapters' missing,
Pasts from prisons,
Past the limits,
White-out all the bad decisions,
Whole time I'm just trying,
Write you back to precision.
The intuition,

Before you ever folded or bended,
You hit every goal you envisioned
Never let the deck set your limit
You hit every goal you envisioned
Never let the deck set your limit

What hurts me more than all of the things I've been through,
Is knowing that you're still out there,
Battling your addiction too.

I Cry

Lord I cry,
Every single one of my tears went dry,
Trying to battle this addiction that's inside.
Writing her all the prescriptions to get high,
Just to get by.
Lord I cry.

Separated

Counting the short steps.
Thought she'd walk like her insides,
Cerebral palsy.

An absent eardrum,
Her strut is a loud silence,
Quicksand in motion.

I hear her empty,
Treads light with a heavy heart,
It rattles like keys.

She knocks like sorry,
Apology accepted,
I never answer.

Power Rangers

It's funny how life's situations change us.
We used to be best friends but now we act like strangers.
I remember when we were gamers,
Used to run around the house pretending to be power rangers.
I was the red one and you would be the blue.
When we combined our powers there wasn't anything we couldn't do.
Remember that?
It's morphin time!
Remember back?
Go, go power rangers.
What happened to us?
It seemed like when we grew up,
The more we grew apart.
I scratched my head trying to figure out when it all started.
It must have been that early Saturday morning,
We sat in front of the TV screen.
Wouldn't eat breakfast until we saw the Power Rangers team.
Suited up in the whole costume and it wasn't even Halloween,
They were pjs.
We would slide around the house arguing over which ranger was better.
Mom stopped us and said you're strongest when you worked together.
We overlooked that,
The words exchanged we never took back.
Our bond broke because of an act.
Make-believe.
How could this tv show make you believe, in colors,
More than your own color, more than your brother?
Told me you'd kill me if I wore the wrong color,

Like we didn't come from the same mother.
Or was it that not so merry Christmas when they made a mistake?
Switched our presents a twist of fate, your eyes filled with hate.
It was the Red Ranger Action-Figure.
You're tears blinded you.
You couldn't see I just wanted to be like you.
I disliked blue, I said I did because you did.
I wanted to be the blue Power-Ranger kid.
Somewhere down the line you let hate fill your head,
Until you worshiped red.
I used to make excuses for your ignorant behavior,
Help me understand.
How do you hide behind colors, and let it claim your identity.
Walked out on your family.
What I can I do to get you to turn back,
Keep you from slipping back, your heart from fading black?
How can you act like Black doesn't exist?
Do you hear that?
That's your bloods calling,
No, this your blood calling.
We can't let them win that easy.
These tears have no color,
Our love has no color.
I'm not going to sit back and let you choose the Bloods over blood,
while the bloods take another blood brother from me.

Breaking Point

Ever felt alone in a crowded room?
Wishing that your mind was as hollow as these walls.
Then maybe someone could hear the screaming,
On the other side of a convoluted smile.
Ever watched the sun set?
Sit locked until your retinas burn and blur?
Spots in your vision,
Faded.
As he feels,
Like a blotch.
A dead man struts.
His pupils remind me of new moons,
Absent,
Like my empathy,
Like neglected bills.
I have problems of my own.
I have a dog,
Waiting to be walked today,
Clawing at the front door,
Dying for a release.
My phone rang seconds before it happened,
I ignored it,
Opened the front door.
A man committed suicide today.
Just like everyone else,
I sat and watched.

Maybe I Will Return

A raven never forgets its favorite tree.
Maybe I will return,
When the wind is still,
Humid and dry.
As a gust or storm,
Tramp them in my eye.
When they welcome me back,
Filling empty space with begging croaks,
They interpret as death.
Maybe they are right,
To take root and be still.
As eager as I am to return to my favorite tree,
With an empty nest it welcomes me.

Two Truths, Both Lies

A Friendship of Deceit

My old roommate was a liar.
I used to back his stories as if they were true.
I guess that by association,
this made me a liar too.
Perhaps I was too gullible.
My ears, worn brown paper bags,
His stories, water.

The low uneven spin of a box fan pushed stale are in lazy circles around our dorm room. The walls—a faded beige, scuffed with the ghosts of furniture long removed, like the echoes of his past exaggerations. Samir sat at the other end of the couch, one arm draped over his forehead like a man burdened by the weight of too many untold legends.

"Catherine was smart and sexy. Temptation in the flesh," he said, his voice thick, with the kind of nostalgia only liars could manufacture. The way he stretched out "Temptation," slow and deliberate, like a name she could have answered to.

"Everybody used to lie and say they were with her, but she was always my girl. We used to fight a lot, but sex was always the best. You know it's good when it's always the best. You ever had a woman that good, lil bro?"

He didn't even wait for me to respond. Instead, a smirk carved into his face like he already knew the answer.

"That's how I know you don't get no buns!" He slapped his chest, laughing in that way that filled the room.

Did I ever tell you about the time when..."

With Samir, there was always a long pause. He took a deep inhale, filling his lungs as if he were gathering the ingredients of a masterpiece before letting them spill out in the form of a lie.

"I was arrested for having sex too loud?"

My eyes widened like a reflex to an old trick you've seen too many times. I gave him a skeptical stare, the kind that sat halfway between amusement and exhaustion. If I told him I had already heard it, he'd insist it was worth hearing again, so I chose to stay silent, losing the fight to maintain focus. Somewhere into the story my mind drifts...

The words became background noise, blending into the hum of the fan, the occasional creak of the old arm of the couch. My focus unraveled, slipping through the cracks in the conversation.
Somewhere into the story, my mind drifted...

***

The couch, a sinkhole slowly shrouding my reality. I allowed my body to groove to the band playing in the hazy glimpses behind my eyelids, letting the music slip between the seconds of darkness. 'These lies - will catch up to you one day.

My left foot tapped on the loose floorboard. My lungs, a saxophone, shaping the rhythm in unspoken song. My arms shaped an imaginary guitar, I strummed along.

'These lies will catch up to you one day.
so fast you can't run away.'
The fall as big as the climb,
Lose the dollars, at the drop of a dime.

In due time your future will pay,
For the crimes you're committing today.
These lies...will catch up to you one day.
No matter how fast you can't run away.

You can't keep going on like this moving,
You'll never win when you're stuck on losing.
These lies..."

"Listen man, I'm at the good part." Samir's voice became a wailing siren, disrupting the jam session in my head.

I shoved my new song inside of the nearest closet in the back of my mind, as if a parent just walked into the bedroom of a disobedient punished teenager, hiding her boyfriend.

"I'm listening." I fire back.

"I bent her over, head out of her bedroom window." he belches as he grabs two bottles of water out of the mini refrigerator.

I challenged, "I thought you were in the kitchen."

"We started in the kitchen, all over the table, we almost broke the table, then we moved to the bedroom." I am amazed at how fast he recovered his story.

He continued, "We were going at it, all over each other like wild animals. She was screaming loud, kept telling me how good it felt.

Then she just started crying. I'm not talking about silent tears, she was boo-hoo crying. That's when I started going deeper."

"Did you at least check on her?" I jump, frightened by the pitch of my own voice.

"Now I really know you don't get no cheeks! Lil bro, women cry all the time, but you have to know how to decipher what they are really saying. Half the time, they don't even know what they want. Slow down usually means go faster, and stop usually means don't stop."

"That really means rape, man seriously, you can't be out here doing that," slamming my open hands down as the table wobbles. I silently stumble upon a graveyard of truths.

"Can't take a joke! Don't f-ck up my story trying to go feminist on me. Let me finish before you charge me officer." He laughed while jumping back into his story without missing a step.

"I had her digging her nails in my back." He learned forward, "Look I still have the marks." The same marks he uses whenever he tells the story about the time he crashed his motorcycle. I don't believe he ever owned a motorcycle. I often wonder about the real story behind the scratches on his back.

"The next thing I know, I hear her knocking on my front door. I'm thinking it was the food delivery. I threw on some pants and ran downstairs. The police cuffed me as soon as I opened the door. They didn't even read me my rights. It's all good, because they had to let me go."

I looked down at my flashing cell phone. The screen reads Mindy (music notes and heart emoji), "My girl Mindy is calling me man. I forgot I have to go pick her up." I moved toward the door relieved exiting so quickly that I don't remember saying goodbye.

Somehow, listening to his delusions made me feel like a liar. Our lease was on its last couple of days and Samir chose to move back in with his parents.

After he moved out, I found his journal on the window seal. That night I sat on the floor in the middle of what used to be a cluttered room, reading his entries aloud.

Around the furthest
corner in the most
honest heart, exercises a
lie waiting for its
moment to protect its
home.

Fear Knot

I'm afraid to admit that I'm afraid of you.
Sleep with the lies on, because the truth is darkness and that scares
me.
Like you do,
The bump in the night.
The horror,
The ghost of everything righteous.
I fear all that will become of me.
The what if,
Greater than faith.
I believe in what I create and control.
I conceive all that is real.
Once gave the world a chance to lead,
The lies remain,
To protect the gain,
I choose
Self-preservation,
Create all,
Believe all,
Fear knot!

Guilt

Stole a drum set from some random garage last night.
Earned enough to almost forget,
Your favorite color is red.
Would've made the perfect gift.

.
I lost the locket.
The picture of you smiling
helped counter the marathon of memories - the night I left
made a left turn
ended right - at the bottom of the bottle.

I see fuzzy images of you crying,
Looks like laughter when I hold it in the light

The Music is loud, I know this tune.
I just can't make it out of this song
Still, I sing along,
"Ever-been-in-love-
     Without a heart?"

The Experiment

Vanessa has a heart like science,
Doesn't believe in love because it doesn't make sense.
Since I've shown emotion,
She's monitored my action levels,
Taken samples of our conversation,
And she's begun to run tests.

She says, I call too much.
I told her that I like to hear her voice.
She told me to stop.
Already she's had too much exposure,
And not sure if I am hazardous.

She's been fed lies like airborne particles.
Dealt with too many fissile emotions,
Believes that a good man is a mirage in her desert of distrust.
Draws a hypothesis that I won't be around much longer.
Checks my cell phone messages to support her theory.

I know a girl with a heart like science,
Einstein as her guard dog.
She once dissected my smile and told me that it was sneaky.
Put a microscope on me every time a cute girl walks by.

Her last boyfriend cheated,
The boy before her didn't return calls.
Her daddy hungover, an overdose of mistakes.
Side effects include insecurity,
a lack of patience, and an Isaac Newton complex.
Gravity lets her high emotions fall,
But she will never allow herself to fall in love.

I know a girl with a heart like science,
Einstein as her guard dog.
She is drawn to me.
Says I have the personality of ten thousand electrons.
She hasn't seen someone illuminate with more success,

Sense artificial light.
Won't get close to me,
Just enough to take samples,
And draw conclusions.

I talk about my feelings,
She changes the subject.
Treats my heart like a hot spot.
Distance in between us when we walk.
Like holding my hand was a health hazard.

I promise you will fail,
Every time you test subjects, like test subjects.
I'm not a f-cking experiment!

Don't blame me for the corporations you let pollute your heart.
You have the mind of a malnourished willow-
Trees can't produce fruit in the stiffness
that has settled beneath your ribcage.
Vanessa, there exists a habitat too inhumane for heartache,
It baffles the reason like a kiloton of correction
exploding in your spleen.

Vanessa, you will never know love,
Until you remove your heart
From this
Latency -
Period!

Innocent

I was her heart murmur.
Gave her an extra beat when I wasn't satisfied,
Stopping her flow like cardiac-
Arrest.
Breaking chains to her menstrual
cycles,
Dry like deserts.
Her eyes rain with regrets,
In a hail of heart attacks.
Watering weeping willows in her fourth chamber.
Trying to put out wildfires,
Heartburns.
Maybe next time she won't love so innocently.

On Sight

Some armies believe nights make better fights,
My soldier is trained to attack on sight.
On hills we battle to make the peaks, peak,
Valleys we travel to bring floods from the deep.
We have slain many beasts wildly they come,
Chase chairs challenge, makes the capture more fun.

Blood may be shed, when no armor is worn.
We will concur until white flags are drawn.
The top of the day, or noon whisk away,
The moon of the night provides perfect light.
You come heavy, come here, come now, come fight.
My soldier is ready to attack on sight.

Smoke

Get used to the smoke.
Let it fill your lungs and sting your eyes.
There's no getting rid of it.
Not in a story about forbidden lovers,
Fucking on a burning mattress.
His loins extinguished the fire.
Her forest now drenched.
Still burned feels beautiful,
Exposed.
White clouds.
Clitoris tingles,
Like flames.
He jumps,
At any chance to rescue her again.
He only knows how to be a hero.
Fight fires like his father,
even if it's not his house burning.
The faceless girl, with the gasoline hips,
and a match for lips is on fire.
He will save her,
Get used to the smoke.

Nobody
Asked Me

I Wish They Would!

The night's got a funny way 'bout it. You can lose yourself all day long, but soon as that sun dips down, that's when the real light turns on—inside yourself, I mean. That's when you find everything you been lookin' for. When the whole world hushes up, seems like that's when your mind gets to runnin' the most. Leastways, that's when mine does.

Now, I ain't old-old, but in my seventy-six years, I never could figure why folks get so spooked by the dark. Then, just last night, soon as I flipped them lights off—BAM! It hit me. Plain as day. Folks ain't scared of the dark. They scared of bein' alone in it. Don't matter how many years you rack up, that fear just don't shake loose. This world'll have you thinkin' you oughta love everybody 'cept yourself. Ain't never satisfied with what the Good Lord gave you. Always tellin' you to change yourself, but love other folks just the way they are. Now, if you ask me, that don't make a lick of sense. But ain't nobody askin' me, and Lord, I sure wish they would.

Katherine's too old to be that young and too young to be that dumb. I watched that girl grow up from a snot-nosed young'un to a real beauty—a bonafide princess. Had the prettiest eyes a girl ever had. Looked green sometimes, but she put her hand to the Bible, they was light brown. Now, either she don't know her colors, or my doctor was right—I really am goin' blind.

Anyway, Kat used to be well-mannered. Always had a "yes, ma'am" or a "no, sir" ready when speakin' to her elders. That let me know she come from a good household. Even though her momma and daddy didn't have the best relationship, Kat was a good little girl.

Her parents used to fuss and holler somethin' awful 'cause her daddy had a bad habit—man couldn't hold onto a dollar to save his life. More nights than not, he'd lose his whole paycheck down at the pool hall gamblin'.

Now, Kat's momma used to be a real looker. I'd watch her walk by and just chuckle at how all the menfolk turned their heads, tryna steal a glimpse of what the Lord blessed her with. Had that smooth kinda skin that didn't need nothin' extra.

Then one day, she started wearin' all that makeup to church. Be sittin' there in the pew with them big ol' sunglasses on, thinkin' she was foolin' somebody. I called 'em battered women shades. Lord knows who she thought she was hidin' from, 'cause everybody knew. Wasn't no secret her man took his temper out on her. Them bruises stood out like a dirt stain on a weddin' gown.

But even with all that, I gotta say—they still did a fine job raisin' that girl. Kat didn't talk much. Wasn't raised to be loose with her tongue. And she sure wasn't out there actin' a fool like these fast-tailed girls nowadays. She was 'bout seventeen at the time, and you wouldn't catch her tangled up in nobody else's business—too busy mindin' her own.

I used to wonder when she was gonna leave that house and start a family of her own. I'd say, "Girl, as pretty as you are, these men oughta be throwin' themselves at your feet. You 'bout ripe now. You best not wait too long. Don't you want some babies?

She'd look up at me with them big ol' eyes and say, "Yes, ma'am, I do want children. I want a big family, but I wanna finish school first."

Well, that 'bout said all that needed sayin' right there. All I could do was shake my head and let out a, "Well, bless your heart."

She just smiled—big and bright as the sun—then kept right on walkin'.

She was so focused and determined when she went off to college. And I know she was doin' well, 'cause her momma made sure everybody and their cousin knew that Kat was on a full scholarship—tuition paid in full, not a dime outta pocket. Said she was studyin' journalism. Smartest girl in the city, how her momma tells it.

After that, I didn't see much of her 'cept for the holidays, when the schools let out. She'd come home for Thanksgiving and Christmas, sittin' at the table like she never left. And Lord, things seemed a whole lot more peaceful then.

Then finally, she met a nice young man in college and got married. I almost started to wonder if she ever made time for herself. Always workin', always studyin', always pushin' forward. I was happy for her—truly, I was—until I found out things weren't goin' too well.

I saw her one day, and my heart near 'bout broke clean in two. She was wearin' them same ol' battered-woman shades her momma used to wear. Wouldn't surprise me none if it was the exact same pair.

Now, there was a time when Kat was expectin'. She had that

glow—y'know the one. That expectant mother's joy, talkin' 'bout paintin' the nursery and pickin' out baby names. But life's got a cruel way of throwin' curveballs, and Kat got hit with a big one.

She carried that baby full term, nursin' dreams and hopes with every little kick and flutter. But when the time came... that baby didn't make it. Doctors said it was the stress, the kind that don't just weigh on your mind—it settles in your bones, it pulls at your spirit 'til you don't know what's left of yourself.

I remember seein' Kat after that. Her eyes was filled with tears that no words could heal, no prayer could lift. She held onto that pain like a sacred burden, carryin' it with her everywhere she went.

Grief got a way of puttin' years on a person, drainin' the life right outta 'em. And you could see it clear as day in that girl—she looked like a piece of her done died right along with that baby.

Nobody asked me what I thought about it. And Lord knows I wish they would.

Well, I reckon folks change. Life's like that sometimes. But seein' Kat all beat up and worn out, that hurt somethin' fierce. I couldn't shake the worry from my heart, couldn't stop thinkin' 'bout the girl she used to be, the girl who used to light up a room just by walkin' in it. I wanted to do somethin', say somethin'—but truth be told, I didn't rightly know what to do.

So, I did what any good neighbor would do. I kept an eye out, checked in on her when I could. But it seemed like she was slippin' further and further away, keepin' to herself more and more.

Then one day, I saw her packin' up her car. And I knew.

She had that look in her eye—the kind that says a person's done had enough, done made up their mind. There was somethin' strong in the way she moved, like she wasn't just leavin'—she was startin' over. And I felt it then, a little stirrin' of hope in my heart.

Turns out, Kat was headin' out west, startin' fresh in a whole new town. Said she was done with all the mess, done lettin' somebody else call the shots.

I watched her drive away, feelin' a mix of sadness and pride. Sad to see her go, but proud—proud that she found the strength to leave. 'Cause sometimes, the hardest thing a person can do is walk away.

She took off those battered woman shades, set 'em on the porch rail, and drove away—

The only thing that's darker than the bruises, is believin' you have to wear 'em.

Accident At Heart

I'll speed down the avenues of my heart with hate,
Discontinue the use of my signals and breaks.
Expel my devotion as i step on the gas,
Begin the realization that this feeling won't last.

Since my heart is broken,
my soul can't be set free.
If you have a love token,
Please spare one for me.

I've tried to do what's best for me,
Wised up and moved on,
Every road that I travel down,
I seem to be going wrong.

Now forget it,
I can't seem to get it.
I speed down the avenues of my heart with hate,
Discontinue the use of my signals and breaks.
Every red light and stop sign I see I fly pass,
Since my heart is broken, I'm waiting to crash.

Stillborn

*I await new hope to glimmer through the shades of sorrow, in the
midnight hour.*
Await spider crabs of light to tickle life back into a newborn.
This is not another abortion poem,
I wanted to die.
crowing me into a world that would never accept me as king.
Don't you dare shed a single tear for me, mother.
*There is a piece of you that was glad that God's mail had a return
address.*
I was the one package that you were not ready to sign on anyway.
I heard the chaos behind the jazz music you used to play.
Don't play me, mother.
You felt your water break premature,
like fish trying to commit suicide,
Jumping up out of the sea,
I see you mother,
Detached from your umbilical cord.
Pressing your weight against me as if I weigh nothing.
I heard door slams,
Loud screams,
Sizzling secrets of sorrow.
I could hear your thoughts,
*But you never took the time to hear the grass grow on the other side
of silence.*
Can you hear me not mother?
You used to be an artist, a painter to be exact.
*The news of my conception left your mind like a landscape on an
unsupported canvas.*
You used to paint your life,
Beautiful,
Like the bond of mankind after a natural disaster,
Beautiful like a virgin's orgasm.
I was a dampen on your imagination like dreamless nights,
Like science to religion,
*Like a child told to leave behind her imaginary friend on her seventh
birthday.*

I watched rainbows fade into the sky,
The sky fade into the clouds,
And the clouds fade like my pulse.
This is my suicide note stitched to your placenta.
I lifted weights trying to be strong for you,
Lifting wait, trying to be patient.

I don't know how many nights I was in here wishing I was there,
to make your worries disappear into my arms.
To make your worry disappear like my arms
I would have been an arm full of worry,
For that reason, I could not let you hold me.
Lets face it,
This pregnancy was a car crash, and I didn't want to be born a
wreck.
So consider it a birthday gift that I was
Still-born.

Her Story

She wears words like stained sheets,
Tossed by a stubborn perfectionist.
Last time she finished a book, yesterday but could not remember
how it started.
Wants the world to know how beautiful she is on the inside,
Invites guests to explore her like a museum.
Gives a discount on admission,
As long as you leave something behind.
Tell her she is worthy of decoration,
That you can still preserve art on wet walls.
Tell her that her story makes sense,
Even though the climax is hollow.
Tell her that she is a best-seller,
A national inquirer,
Tell her that you will make sure that her sports illustrated,
On the front page of a mother 20 years before she gives birth.
Tell he that you will make a class of it,
That you will teach women how to raise women.
Collect her dirty stained sheets,
Bind them into the hands of a million first ladies.
Teach them how to complete thoughts in the right direction,
So that they would be explored in museums.
Change the world back into proper rotation.
The only thing Her story is missing,
you.

She Is

On the other side of the country.
A familiar distance,
Reminds her of home,
Of her reflection.
She is,
Not what she does,
A midnight train ride on the sunny side of regret.
She is protection.
A double barrel sawed-off shotgun, close range with no trigger,
She is no trigger.
I can't pull her.
Still the first weapon I reach for,
If ever called to war.
There is no war.
No reason to be armed,
No need to shoot powerful blanks,
Can't hit a missing target,
I still like to stay sharp,
Because she is.

In The Rough

Plucked roses reveal swollen thorns
See beyond flattery

Compliments are not visas
But for you they work like master cards
You approved him too much credit
Now you're in debt

Please tell me
How can a diamond be so poor?
When did you lose clarity?

You say be free
But you chose to remain in the rough
I'm not mad at him
Before him
You were a slave without a master
A damsel disaster, under duress
saved by a bastard, his hands perfectly grip your neck

Yea he may be doing you wrong now,
Before him, you were playing hopscotch on a busy freeway

They say god helps those who help themselves
I must have been a fool to think that i was a better god

After he left
I stayed and watched you go back to where you were before him
In the rough

Goodbye

In the shadowed dance of our entangled fate,
My world unravels, a delicate date.
Blame not assigned, the fault is mine to bear,
No pretense of joy when you're not there.
Together we dance in sorrow's embrace,
An encore of DeJa'Vu of the first I love you, we chase.
Perhaps, in parting, new horizons we'll find,
A canvas where destinies are artfully entwined.
Here we stand, the threshold of the living,
Withhold tears, our story, beautifully written.
Save those tearful jewels, for a future untold,
Goodbye, we wrap where we stand wrapped,
in a bittersweet fold.

Hotwired

The Connection

A circuit is a closed pathway for electricity.
Every electrical appliance whether it is battery operated or if
you plug it in, has a circuit.

Circuits work because of moving electrons.
All circuits have three main parts; a power source, a
conducting path, and a load.

Every creature on this planet is a part of a circuit.
We are all individual power sources, looking to conduct a
path into someone that will use the electricity.
This is a story about the day I found my load.

I stood in line at the coffee shop, checking my watch for what
felt like the hundredth time. 8:43 am. If I hurried, I might just
make it to work on time for my 9 am start.

As the line inched forward, I mentally calculated how long
it would take to order, receive my drink, and rush to the
office. The aroma of freshly brewed coffee filled the air,
tempting me to abandon my plans and just savor the moment.

When it was finally my turn to order, I quickly rattled off my request to the barista, trying to sound confident despite my rush. "A medium Iced Caramel Mocha Latte with a warmed coffee cake, please."

"That sounds delicious," a voice behind me said. "Make that two."

I turned to see who had spoken, and my breath caught in my throat when I saw her smiling back at me. It wasn't just any smile; it was a smile that seemed to shimmer with a kind of ethereal glow, like moonlight dancing on the surface of a lake. Her lips curved upwards in a way that was both captivating and enigmatic, hinting at a world of secrets and stories.

I found myself unable to look away. It was as if she had cast a spell on me with her smile.

"Destiny," I said, my heart at the climax of a symphony. "I... I ..." I struggled to find my words.

"I miss you too Kai," she replied softly.

As we stood there, I noticed the way her eyes flickered with longing and passion. It was like a spark igniting between us, setting off a chain reaction of excitement and connection. I knew that this encounter was unlike any other.

"That's eight dollars and forty-nine cents," the barista's voice broke the spell, pulling me back to the reality of the coffee shop.

I fumbled for my wallet, my mind still partially lost in the moment with Destiny. As I handed the barista a ten-dollar bill, I glanced back at the line and realized that it had almost doubled in size. How long had we been locked into each other's eyes?

"Keep the change," I said absentmindedly, my attention already drifting back to Destiny.

As we collected our drinks and found a table, I couldn't shake the feeling that our meeting was more than just a coincidence. It was as if the universe had conspired to bring us together, and I was intrigued.

We sat adjacent but our knees close enough to share the eruption of goosebumps. Our bodies welcomed the intrusion, time matched a slowing heartbeat. The world around us faded into a blur. Our drinks sat forgotten, the melting ice discolored the top of the cups, while we sat, perfectly blended in each other's eyes.

There was no need for words. Our eyes spoke a language of their own, a language of understanding. We stared, lost in the current. I could see the flicker of emotions in her eyes, mirrored in my own. There was a softness, a tenderness in her gaze that made my heart swell with affection.

It was as if we were in our own little bubble, cocooned from the rest of the world. The hustle and bustle of the coffee shop faded away, replaced by the sound of our hearts beating in unison.

As the minutes passed, I knew that this was a moment I would never forget. It was a silent conversation, but it was the most beautiful conversation I had ever had.

I broke the silence with a heavy heart, "I'm in a engaged,' I said. My words landed like gravity somehow, we remained on the moon.

"I see," Destiny replied, her stare continued.

"Congratulations. How long?"

"Together for three years, and I asked her to marry me three months ago."

Her gaze was challenging. Somehow everything around us

melted away, we were alone in the room.

"Do you believe that you are making the right decision?" Her question landed like a home burglary during a holiday dinner party.

My defenses were down. I managed to let out, "I... am," As sure as my dishonesty would allow. I was as unsettled as the melting ice in our cups.

Destiny leaned forward, her eyes locked on mine,

Her question lingered in the air, forcing me to confront my own feelings. Destiny had opened a door to a conversation with a truth I had been avoiding.

It had been more than five years since we had seen each other.

"Where do you work?" Destiny asked, breaking the silence between us.

"Around the corner," I replied. "And what about you?"

"Small world, my office is two blocks away." We had been seconds away from bumping into each other for three years.

We were silent, as we walked to her office, stealing glances at each other. I noticed a city bus honking at a random pedestrian crossing outside of the crosswalk. We gave each other a passionate embrace before she walked into work.

***

"I'm done with that report you asked me to finish. Do you want me to leave it on your desk?" my coworker, Angie, asked.

"Sure, Angie," I replied without looking up, my gaze fixed on the screen. I had finally begun to collect my thoughts and concentrate. I couldn't even recall the walk to work that morning.

"Omari, you've been daydreaming since you floated in here this morning at 9:30. It must be nice to be the boss," Angie teased.

"Just happy, that's all," I replied, unable to contain my smile.

I glanced down at my phone and saw a text message:

'Lunch?'

I texted back
'Sure'

'I'm downstairs,'

"If anyone is looking for me, tell them I took my lunch. Yes, leave the report on my desk," I instructed Angie. I grabbed my coat and rushed to the elevator, my mind racing with thoughts of Destiny.

'Wait, how did you get my number?'
I never pressed send.

As I stepped out the door, there she was, waiting for me with lunch in hand. We hugged with so much passion, like we were two magnets drawn irresistibly together. I didn't know how we managed to pull apart.

"Thank you for the food."

"No problem. I ordered Carribean food and figured you might want some. Look, I usually go home to eat but if you don't want to, I understand." while holding up her ring finger.

"We can go to your place, where do you live?" I shot back.

"5 minutes away, and we can take your car." Destiny responded.

***

We arrived at Destiny's house and walked inside, the air thick with desire and anticipation. After placing our food down, she turned to me, her eyes smoldering with passion, and we shared a deep, lingering kiss. The touch of her lips against mine sent a jolt of electricity through my body, igniting a fire within me.

A voice in the back of my mind reminded me of the consequences of my actions. I knew deep down that I was wrong, that we had crossed a line that should never have been crossed. But in the heat of the moment, the allure of Destiny was too strong to resist. There I stood, with the weight of my actions pressing down on me, and her lips pressing against mine.

Our bodies danced to the rhythm of our desires, each movement sparking a new wave of pleasure. I traced the lines of her body like a circuit, feeling the electric current that flowed between us. Her skin was a conductor, channeling the heat of our passion.

As we kissed, our lips became electrodes, sparking and igniting a fire that burned hotter with each passing moment. I felt a surge of energy as our bodies pressed together, the voltage of our connection reaching new heights.

I kicked the door shut, sealing us in our own world of ecstasy. We fell onto the couch, our movements synchronized. Every touch sent a shockwave through me, every caress a jolt of pleasure.

We peeled off our clothes, each garment another shallow barrier to be overcome. And then, as our naked bodies met, it was as if a circuit had been completed.

The electricity between us,was palpable, crackling in the air like a storm about to break. A storm that would change our lives forever.

We moved in the frequency of passion and power; each movement, a live wire, raw expression of our connection.

We moved together with an intensity that bordered on the divine, our bodies becoming one in a blaze of ecstasy.

And as we reached the peak of our pleasure, it was like a surge of electricity, coursing through us and leaving us breathless and spent, our bodies humming with the aftershocks of our passion.

The electricity between us, was palpable, crackling in the air like a storm about to break. A storm that would change our lives forever.

We moved in the frequency of passion and power; each movement, a live wire, raw expression of our connection. We moved together with an intensity that bordered on the divine, our bodies becoming one in a blaze of ecstasy.

And as we reached the peak of our pleasure, it was like a surge of electricity, coursing through us and leaving us breathless and spent, our bodies humming with the aftershocks of our passion. We laid bodies entangled, and talked about everything. I felt alive in a way I hadn't in a long time, as if her presence had unlocked something inside me that had been dormant for too long. I looked at my phone and saw two missed calls. It's 7: 00 pm.

"It's getting late. I have to get home," I said, my voice tinged with reluctance. I gathered my things, I felt a pang of guilt creeping in.

"Don't forget your food," she said, handing me the container.

Before I left, I pulled her into a passionate kiss,
savoring the taste of her lips one last time. As I
walked out the door, a sense of longing washed over me.

On the way home, I concocted a story about having to work late, a lie to cover up the truth of where I had really been.

I was struck by a sense of confusion. I felt guilty about having to lie but not about the time we had shared together. There was something about our connection that felt right, despite the circumstances.

I went to work the next day as if nothing had happened. I buried the memory of our passionate encounter deep within me. The guilt lingered, as the flashes of passion made my body shiver like a chill, both thrilling and forbidden.

***

Two weeks went by, and I stayed resolute, resisting the urge to reach out to Destiny. Then, out of the blue, her message popped up:

'Hey, forget about me?'

I knew I had to set things straight.

*'Look, I'm sorry. It was a
Mistake. I'm getting
married. I shouldn't
Have let things go as
far as they did.'*

She responds,

*'Tell me that any part of
what happened between
us really felt wrong, and
I will stop.'*

I stared at Destiny's message, the words pierced through my will and freed my desire. Did any part of what happened between us really feel wrong? I wrestled with the question, the guilt and confusion swirling inside me like a storm.

After a moment of hesitation, I replied, "Every part of it felt wrong. I betrayed my wife, and I betrayed myself. What we did was a mistake, and it can never happen again."

There was no response from Destiny, and I felt a sense of relief mixed with sadness. I had hurt her, and for that, I would always carry a heavy heart. But I knew that I had made the right decision, for my marriage and for my conscience.

She went silent. At that moment, I didn't know what to feel. I was expecting at least some reaction from her. I was sure I had hurt her feelings. Why was I even concerned with hurting her? I tried to bury myself in work, but I couldn't shake off the slight annoyance that lingered.

Then, just when I thought the silence would stretch on indefinitely, a text message popped up on my phone:
'

Lunch? :)

The text!
The spark!
And just like that,
his pulse surged,
pulling him back to where it
all started.
Will he answer this time?

I Christ You

I Christ you,
Bear your sins if I could.
Exchange my life for your salvation. Resurrect myself just to live in
you again. Pay tithes to your womb.
I Joseph you,
Crawl in your belly and sing you to sleep. Hug your pulse,
Pause at your loneliest moment,
Whisper promises of a better tomorrow, Until you follow the voice
inside of you.
I've found heaven inside of you,
And I want to bring you here,
Back to yourself.
To witness the miracles,
Promises unbroken,
Heart,
Before they broke in,
And took everything they thought you had.
The Garden,
Innocence,
Sacrifice,
The Love,
The return,
I Christ you.
Sweet Dreams
Last night I watched you sleep,
Defining grace,
Defying gravity,
As if angels cradled your silhouette.
I laid my future inside your crescent,
Stripped my past at beside,
Exposed to your light.
I plugged my projector into your dreams.
My favorite episodes are interrupted by the commercials,
Where you turn and grab me close.
Sweet dreams.

Sweet Dreams

Last night I watched you sleep,
Defining grace,
Defying gravity,
As if angels cradled your silhouette.
I laid my future inside your crescent,
Stripped my past at beside,
Exposed to your light.
I plugged my projector into your dreams.
My favorite episodes are interrupted by the commercials,
Where you turn and grab me close.
Sweet dreams.

Aftermath

A sunrise after the storm.
A flag raised after a war.
Serenity after a prayer.
The seventh day caught in a twilight zone.
Living the promise of life after, before death,
Before the first sin,
After salvation.

Caught in limbo, like a balanced scale.
Spooning is the proper utensil according to my tongue,
But this tastes better than my favorite bowl of cereal.
Waking up next to you has my innocence of a mountain bike,
Popping wheelies.

My eyes glisten, removing the corners crust,
Crevasse at the base of doubt.
We may get things twisted, but I will never not knot,
Believe in what we have.
The bed as warm as the day we first met,
Passion as hot as morning breath.
The extended stretch, surrendering to the best part of our
day.
The most exciting part of my night?
Anticipating waking up next to you.

No Tale to Folk

A captive, bound to love's unpredictable seas.
My body resonates with the sirens' plea.
A supplicant to an elusive tease,
Waves of passion, intricate and free.
Intertwined, surrendered to the trance.
The movement we find in the motionless dance,
Until the sea settles, judgment, better scope, Witness wisdom wain
when anchors dislodge from the boat.
No folk to tell,
No tale to folk.

Let's

She reads aloud,
In a language unfamiliar to man,
Oxy-metaphoric its familiar to me.
She illustrates the poise of a tamed lion,
Capturing the swiftness of a shooting star.
Sometimes I wonder if she existed in a lifetime before me,
Or if she's just a vision of what has yet to come.
Whatever it may be,
In her eyes I see trinity.
Her tongue,
Is encrypted with hieroglyphics, only my heart can decode it.
She pulsates air into my lungs,
I take her in portions.
I study her,
If she ever asked me what I'm in school for,
I can tell her, I plan to master you.
Talking to you makes me feel like I'm on the edge
of a fantasy.
Let me to travel to new places inside of your soul,
Continents not on this globe,
Let's put maps out of business for not providing directions,
They can't seem to navigate you right.
I'm labeling your heart off as a construction site,
Rebuilding from the disasters your past left.
This was made to last past death.
Let me be your Hear - chitect.
I'll build a fifth chamber made of steal,
With me on the inside.
Let me be lost inside you.
I plan to turn this foreign land into my home.
You can find me bathing in the marrow of your bones.
Let me go where the sweetness lies,
In the center of your juices
I like it there its moist and sticky like quicksand.
Let me sing deeper,
Poking new rhythms into your heartbeat,
Until there's no more me left.

You breathe through me.
The next time you speak, regurgitate my semen,
If any man is bold enough to approach you,
Tell him you don't see men,
You breathe kings.
Let's build a lifeline on the outer limits of time.
Let's unlock the ancestral spirits trapped in your spine
Let's be free when were together,
Let's be love defined.

Embers

Past, a charred coal, I navigate,
a conduit, new vigor for fading embers,
The shadows remember, fighting while fickle and tinder.
Awaiting my departure, I weigh ash,
Sand in the wake of all that's past.
Pen and paper, torch in hand,
Yet shadows still speak, from beyond the sand.
This could be the end, a truth I inscribe,
The language of my heart, the fire thrives.

Encore

A preserved smile as flawless as the day we first met.
Your happiness a broadway spectacular.
Brilliance in a genuine laugh on cue.
There's an unmatched comfort between your lips.
Your joy is God's personal masseuse.
Your face will always have a standing ovation,
Every time it performs- a smile.
Encore!

Mindy Ray
is Music

Music is life, and every soul—music.

Some people are just born with music in their soul. If you put your ear to their chest, their heartbeat makes you want to sing along. If you ever watch how they walk, it's like they're dancing across the keys of a piano. You can catch them rocking back and forth or tapping their feet in tune. You wouldn't be able to hear any music, but they're moved by the song inside their spirit.

That's how I know my granddaughter Mindy-Rae is music. I swear to you, there's a harp in her vocal cords. When she speaks, the flowers lean toward her. A warm honey tone, melted butter, sounds like your favorite sing-along. She loves to talk, and whenever she does, I listen.

A free spirit, the kind that makes her feel comfortable talking to strangers and in front of big crowds. Mindy-Rae always finds a way to bring out the joy inside of folks. Every room she's in feels like home.

She has many friends, but when she's alone, it's just her and Melody. Melody is what she named her all-black acoustic guitar that I surprised her with on her fourteenth birthday. I remember that day clear as anything. I'd been saving up for months, hiding cash in an old coffee can in the back of the pantry. Her birthday fell on a Saturday, and I told her we were going to the music shop in town just to look around. She didn't know.

When we got there, I walked her straight to the back where they kept the guitars. There was this one—all black, smooth as silk, with a sound hole that looked like it could swallow the whole world and sing it back out sweeter.

"Go on," I said. "Pick it up."

She looked at me, confused. "Grandpa, I can't—"

"Pick it up, baby girl."

She did. And the second her fingers touched those strings, I knew. The whole shop went quiet. Even the guy behind the counter stopped what he was doing. She strummed once, just once, and the sound that came out— Lord, it was like every song I'd ever heard all wrapped up in one note.

"She's yours," I told her.

Mindy-Rae's eyes filled with tears. "Grandpa—"

"She's yours," I said again. "And you better name her something good.

And that was that.

I don't think she ever lets Melody out of her sight. Carries her everywhere she goes. Don't ever be shocked if you catch her having full conversations with Melody. When she talks, that guitar talks back.

One night—this was maybe two years ago—I heard her crying in her room. Not loud, just soft, like she didn't want anyone to hear. I stood outside her door, hand on the knob, trying to decide if I should go in or leave her be.

Then I heard Melody.

She was playing this slow, mournful tune, and I swear that guitar was crying right along with her. The notes stretched out long and low, like a voice saying, I know, I know, I'm here. After a while, the song changed. Got brighter. The notes started to dance. And when I peeked through the crack in the door, Mindy-Rae was smiling again, wiping her eyes, whispering something to Melody I couldn't quite hear.

That's when I knew—Melody wasn't just a guitar. She was a alive.

Together, they wrote some of the most beautiful music my aging ears have ever heard.

I used to sit in the front row of every one of her recitals. Every single one. Didn't matter if it was at the school auditorium or some little coffee shop downtown. I was there.

I remember the first time I heard her sing 'Free Fall', this song she's been writing. I don't recall ever hearing anything more beautiful. She was sitting on the porch, and the sun was setting behind her. She closed her eyes and just... played. The neighbor's dog stopped barking. Mrs. Henderson across the street came out onto her porch and just stood there, listening.

When Mindy-Rae finished, there were tears on Mrs. Henderson's face. She didn't say a word. Just nodded and went back inside.

That's when I knew—my granddaughter wasn't just playing music. She was giving people something they didn't even know they needed.

But I'm getting old now. My body doesn't work quite like it used to. My knees ache when I stand too long. My hands shake when I try to button my shirt. My little songbird is always on the go, and it's getting harder to keep up.

I know she has to follow her heart, and her heart is always on some stage a few towns over.

It does get lonely here without her.

She called last Tuesday. Or was it last month? Time moves different now. She said she'd be home soon. "Just one more show, Grandpa."

That's what she always says.

And I always say, "You go on and shine, baby girl. I'll be right here."

I don't tell her that "right here" is getting harder to hold onto.

Sometimes, I don't even know if she's in the house or if my mind is replaying her tune. One day she's here, strumming Melody on the porch, filling the air with sound. The next, she's gone, and the house is so quiet I forget what her voice sounds like.

But then I close my eyes, and I can hear it again. That warm honey tone. That melted butter voice.
I can hear her singing.

I used to sit in the front row of every one of her recitals.
Wait. Did I already say that?

I think I did.

Sometimes I forget what I've said and what I've only thought. The days blend together now. Morning feels like evening. Evening feels like morning. I sit in this chair by the window, waiting for her to come up the driveway, guitar case slung over her shoulder, smile lighting up her face.

But she doesn't come.

Or maybe she did, and I missed it.

I don't know anymore.

I hear her now, playing on the porch. Or maybe that's just the wind. The sound is so faint, like it's coming from far away. Like it's coming from inside me.

She used to say, "Grandpa, when I play, I'm talking to God."

And I'd say, "Well then, tell Him I said—"

I can't remember what I was going to say.

But I know it was something good.

Something about how proud I am. How much light she's brought into this world. How every note she plays feels like a prayer I didn't know I needed to hear.

I close my eyes and listen.

The music is so beautiful.

So soft.

Like a lullaby.

Like coming home.

Mindy-Rae, baby girl, you keep playing. You keep shining.

You tell them all—

Tell them your grandpa said—

Tell them—

REST IN PEACE
GRANDPA DAN
SUNRISE MARCH 9, 1947
SUNSET NOVEMBER 21, 2018.

Music is Life,
and Every Soul - Music!

Grandpa's Last Song

A glass of whiskey on the nightstand,
A guitar by your chair,
Pucking hymns and calloused prayers.
Whistlin in the morning light,
Your boot tapped the rhythm of life.
I can still hear you sing.

You taught me how to find the key,
Not just the music, to what I believe.
Your hum is the voice of the night sky,
Singing hallelujah,
A thousand times before the sunrise.
Your boot tapped the rhythm of life.
I can still hear you sing.

Now I play the guitar you used to hold,
Found melodies in the stories you told.
Pucking hymns and calloused prayers.
Until the next stage, I'll meet you there.
Like old times, you will sing loud,
I'll join in, making you proud.

Keep that guitar strumming, keep that choir strong,
Your boot tapping the rhythm of life, and I will sing along.
I can still hear you sing, I'll sing along.
I can still hear you sing,
Grandpa's last song.

Music has power, It can open your mind and heal you at the same time, set your soul free. A single note transmutes pain, relieves the guards from their post, a cradled storm. My voice, sometimes harp, trumpet, harmonica lately, hazy, been getting better at playing memories into my next days. Been found - ours in Melody, channels in her veins.

When I play, Grandpa Dan is tapping his left foot on the slightly muffled rug, on the floorboard beneath his favorite chair, warn from years of - he's still here. Singing along off-key, sometimes louder than me.

When I play, Grandpa Dan puts his hand on my right shoulder, I correct my form, he nods his head, together we sing along.

But sometimes the quiet of the day envelops my memories, overnights me back to my cold right shoulder, the empty chair across the room, the bald spot on the rug, the rug I can't move. Sometimes the rug and I switch places, we share the same hole. It's hard to keep going when it feels like the only person who truly understood me, fell though whole - stayed in yesterday, and I frozen in time.

For Getting You

I can't afford to stay,
The price is too high.
They want me to pay,
By forgetting you.

Take away my dreams,
Sell them to insomniacs.
I don't need a dime,
Just my time with you.

I won't be punished for getting you,
By forgetting you.
I won't ban you from my mind.
I don't care,
Whatever the cost,
I'll pay the fine.

Call me crazy if you want to,
Call me stupid if you dare.
I don't care if it's true.
I'd rather forget me than forget you.

Take away my heart,
It won't beat the same.
Take away my love,
I'll never love again,
At least not the same way,
I love loving you.

No I won't be punished for getting you,
By forgetting you.
I won't ban you from my mind.
I don't care, whatever the cost,
I'll pay the fines.

Split

I was born on the evening of his departure,
Left on the same train I arrived.
I wonder why he was in such a rush,
When I chose to take my time.
I wish he would have waited for me,
given me a chance to see,
If it's true,
If I belong to you?
Cause I,
Confuse imagination with memory.
I suppose he looks just like me.
It's in the walk,
It's in the talk,
I bet it's all the same.
My imagination leaves me bittersweet,
Just a fantasy replaying.
You could never live up to the hero of you,
That my mind created.

Free Fall

Here's your chance,
To escape to a place,
Where reality is irrelevant.

Here's your out,
From the pain their lies bring,
Make your fantasies definite.

Close your eyes,
Let go,
Free fall,
Past love.

Past the lies,
they've all told.
Free fall,
Past love.

Forget what they told you,
How you're supposed to feel.
Don't let them mold you,
To believe,
it's not real.

Close your eyes,
Let go,
Free fall,
Past love.

Past the lies,
they've all told.
Free fall,
Past love.

Believe

The only thing worse than being afraid to stay,
Is being afraid to leave.
I know how much it still hurts,
The past is behind,
Your future needs you to believe.

How do you hold on,
So tight to thin air?
How do you hold on,
when nothing's there?

The present is a present,
Live and enjoy yourself.
Don't be afraid,
Open your eyes to see.

The only thing worse than being afraid to stay,
Is being afraid to leave.
I know it still hurts,
The past is behind,
The future needs you to believe.

Go DJ

Sometimes I think I should not be this lucky.
I should have ended up on the side of a broken jukebox,
No longer used.
I'm' a scratched record with no label.
A weapon in the wrong hands,
Always in the wrong hands,
Skipped beats,
Jump back and repeat.
A stutter on the wrong line,
The music will always stop playing.

I mourn over the grave of the jukebox.
However broken,
She was always able to fine tune,
Find the tunes that compensated for my mishaps.
Take the abuse for me,
When I did not stay in line.
How did I end up in the hands of an architect?
She knew the blend,
The mix that matched.
She reversed the scratch.
She heard the tune,
When everyone else stopped dancing,
She chose to keep me playing,
The party goes on...

Memories

I want to live inside my memories.
Yesterday please come back to me.
I want to destroy the sun before it has a chance to rise.
So that tomorrow can never come.
If I can't live inside yesterday, today cannot end.
I don't know if my memories will be strong enough to live on
tomorrow.

Hate when I wake up,
Every morning, I rock myself back to sleep.
Back to the dreams I had,
The day before yesterday,
Of how good yesterday could be.
Could we plead insanity if it means a twilight of memories?
I want to live inside my memories.
Let me chase the tears back up your face,
Dive into the pools of your eyes,
Then watch me tickle you until you cry,
For the first time again.

I want to live inside my memories.
Now it makes sense to me,
When I see people wearing clothes from the 80's,
Like they are locked in an era.
Trapped in a time zone,
Free in a zone where time doesn't exist.
I want to be free.
Let's recreate memories,
Have fifty first dates,
An everlasting first kiss,
Walk with me home,
On the other side of the universe.
This never has to end.

Soul Music

I tried to purchase your future from a guy in the back of an alley,
who told me he was down on his luck.
His eyes were as desperate as the desert in mine.
Wet sand hands of an absent father,
I could smell dead-beat on his breath.
Sold me your first candy red apple drum set,
Glistens when the light hits,
Like a bastard sun set at its base.
There's something I have to tell you.
That man was your father.
But this drum set will be a better dad than you than he could ever
be.
It'll teach you about life,
How to stay in line,
A set pace, rhythm,
How to be on time.
How to move away like sound waves.
Like daddy moved away,
Down creeks,
Down streams,
Somewhere downtown he roams free,
Like a murmured verse that never settled down.
Kick, kick, snare, snare, kick, snare.
Play it loud,
Don't miss a beat.
A rusty rhythm to a death audience.
Kick, kick, clash,
Till it rattles eardrums.
Watch them move like they can still hear you.
When they try to sit still,
It'll emit like multiple sclerosis,
Their bones, a bunch of busted amplifiers.
A few dents in the same place,

As if the beat was alive but somebody played it to death.
Kick, kick, snare, snare, kick, snare.
The next time you play,
You will understand the true meaning of a deadbeat.
A bent cymbal of what a father should be.
Beat it until it straitens out,
Like a flat line waiting for a refrain,
A return,
A male's voice instead of a voice mail.
I know that you want to love him.
I know that you are waiting for his DNA to be recomposed
somewhere between the chorus,
and the bridge that you are still longing for him to cross.
On the other end of this composition,
There is a stick figure,
Who can't figure how to stick-
Figures of himself into the memories of another man's son's sticks.
It won't stick.
He gets crazy-
Glue himself to the bottom of the drum,
But broken hearts make dead beats.
Kick, kick, clash.
I hear his boy practicing every night,
Trying to resuscitate love.
Kick, kick, snare, snare, kick, snare,
But broken hearts make dead beats.
Dead beats mean absence from body.
That's soul music.
Soul music has the power to make things reappear. The beat of a
broke heart.
Kick, kick, snare, snare, kick, snare,
Never stop playing that soul music
Soul music, everyone can dance to.

Jamal Tyson Hinnant is an international award-winning poet, best-selling author, and playwright. With a Masters of Arts in Urban Education and fifteen years of experience in education and public speaking, he has made appearances across five continents and dozens of states in the U.S., using his story to inspire resilience, enhance productivity, and guide individuals toward success.

As the founder and CEO of Live the Dream LLC, he supports independent artists globally. He has partnered with MTV, PBS, MSG, and UPN networks, with his work airing on multiple radio stations. As a consultant, Jamal collaborates with EdTech startups and nonprofit organizations, shaping the future of education while empowering organizations and professional speakers worldwide.

www.ingramcontent.com/pod-product-compliance
Lightning Source LLC
Chambersburg PA
CBHW030553030726
47495CB00004B/1232